Scrawny
the Classroom Duck

By Susan Clymer
Illustrated by Stella Ormai

A
LITTLE APPLE
PAPERBACK

SCHOLASTIC INC.

New York Toronto London Auckland Sydney

ISBN 0-590-43729-1

Text copyright © 1991 by Susan Clymer.
Illustrations copyright © 1991 by Scholastic Inc.
All rights reserved. Published by Scholastic Inc.
APPLE PAPERBACKS is a registered trademark of Scholastic Inc.

21 20 19 18 17 16 15 14   5 6/9

Printed in the U.S.A.   40

First Scholastic printing, April 1991

For my father,
Frank T. Clymer,
with love.

1

First Egg Cracks

With an extra loud crack, the duck's bill poked its way out of the smallest egg.

"I saw the duck!" John yelled. He had his face so close to the incubator that his nose touched the warm glass. "I saw our duck *first*!!"

Immediately eighteen other children stopped adding up numbers. They dropped their pencils or chalk and raced to surround the incubator. Elizabeth "accidentally" knocked over Nathan's colored pencils like she always did. Andrew climbed over Allie's desk rather than going around. He left a dusty footprint on her desktop. "Whoooeeee!" Andrew cried.

John poked the button that activated the stopwatch on his watch.

"Stop pushing," Mary begged. She was sitting beside John, trying to write 11:06 A.M. in her *Duck Journal*.

"The egg *is* cracked!" Emily exclaimed. The tiny beak poked through again. "I can see its egg tooth." Emily liked using scientific terms. The egg tooth was the hard pointed tip on the beak of a newborn. The duckling used it to poke out of the shell.

"What if this baby dies?" Elizabeth screeched. Everybody groaned, and Elizabeth started sniffling louder.

"John," Ms. Saunders said.

John heard the soft, steely voice of his teacher even through all the bedlam. He flushed. He and Mary were supposed to be *quietly* observing the egg and writing in their journals while the rest of the third-grade class finished math. John could feel his ears turning red . . . bright red. He looked up at Ms. Saunders's brown eyes, which were usually friendly. "I'm sorry that I yelled."

The duck tapped three times in a row, then stopped as if exhausted.

"Children in the front kneel down so those in the back can see," Ms. Saunders ordered. "And Elizabeth, *stop* that wailing." By now Elizabeth had worked herself up almost to the hiccuping and shivering stage.

John stared again at the littlest egg of the three. No

movement. The whole class had been observing the eggs for ages. Last week the teacher had candled them. She had turned out all the lights in the room. Then she had held the eggs up one by one in front of the projector light, so that the children could see shadows of what was going on inside the eggs. Ms. Saunders was certain she'd seen this littlest embryo kick.

"Now," the teacher whispered into the silence. "We will all be on our quietest best behavior. You wouldn't like being born with twenty hooligans watching."

As if the duck heard her, it chirped for the first time . . . a tiny, tiny sound. John caught his breath in wonder. Then the duck began furiously tapping, pushing up bits of shell.

First the duck tapped a long straight crack more than halfway around the egg, the way John did when he was cracking eggs on the side of the counter to make cookies. Then the egg heaved open. John caught a glimpse of soggy yellow feathers before the egg closed back up. The egg heaved again. This time the duck managed to stick one wet wing out. It had been twenty minutes and thirty seconds exactly since the duck had first poked its beak through the shell.

"Come on, baby," Mary whispered.

The duck heaved itself up again. Tiny webbed feet uncurled so it could stand. The baby creature lifted its head upright for the first time. Then it fell, its pink neck resting along the next egg.

"It's so scrawny!" John exclaimed.

Andrew giggled. "Scrawny, that's what we should call him."

John looked up at the other boy, horrified. Before he could reply, Ms. Saunders said, "Scrawny's a fine name. Scrawny usually means skinny, little, and strong." She tapped John's and Mary's shoulders. "You agree, Mary? You two were the first to see him."

Mary smiled her agreement.

"Welcome, Scrawny," Allie crooned.

John couldn't manage to speak. He hadn't meant to give the duck a terrible name. He would never in a million years give anything a silly name. This was John's first year at this school. So far, he'd managed to keep his own name a secret. Ms. Saunders knew, but she'd never told. John's parents had named him to honor all the nationalities and religions in his family. He was their baby. His name was John Frederick Felix Elijah Forest. He guessed his old English ancestors used to live in the forest. That's how he'd gotten his last name. Elijah was for his Jewish grandmother, so his dad's side of the family wouldn't feel left out. Felix was for his mother's French father, and Frederick for her German grandmother. John was a good Catholic name, to honor the French Catholics.

Luckily, there weren't many Catholic boys' names that started with an *F*. His parents had thought about Francis with an *i*, but one of his sisters was already Frances with an *e*. Both of his parents liked *F*'s, except on his report card . . . as the family joke went. Anyway, his mother had named him John Frederick Felix Elijah Forest.

The baby duck spread its wings and stood up. It wobbled out of the last of its shell, chirping. John was certain that Scrawny looked right at him.

The class cheered.

"I'll make it up to you," John whispered. "I promise."

2

Lonesome Duck

"The important thing is that we have Scrawny," Ms. Saunders announced the next morning. She smiled. Then she blew her nose and dabbed at the corner of one eye.

John sat on the edge of his seat. So did every other child in the room.

"When I arrived this morning, I found our second duck dead," Ms. Saunders continued. "It had pushed its way out of the shell, but it must have been too weak to survive."

John swallowed. Last night, he'd told his parents all about Scrawny... their classroom duck. Now their *only* classroom duck. The third egg had never moved, and John knew it should have by now. The 4-H Club had warned them that sometimes happened to duck and chicken eggs.

"We'll take the last egg apart during recess tomorrow," Ms. Saunders said, "so we can see at what stage the embryo stopped developing. Anyone who wishes may stay inside to watch."

Scrawny peeped.

That was too much for Mary. She started sniffling. Andrew joined her, then half the class was crying, including Ms. Saunders. John rubbed at his own eyes. Elizabeth drummed her heels and wailed.

To John's surprise, Ms. Saunders didn't get upset at Elizabeth for causing a scene. Instead, she handed around an extra box of tissues. "Fine sight we make."

"Ms. Saunders?" Emily asked quietly. She wore brown corduroy overalls with her hair braided to her waist. When the teacher nodded at her, Emily continued. "Ducks need company, right? I mean, they aren't soli — " She stumbled over the scientific word. "Ducks aren't solitary animals, are they?"

John wished he'd thought of that question. At home, Mom always said that asking good questions was a sign of great intelligence. But Dad said that thinking up solutions was more important. John raised his hand. "Someone could stay with Scrawny every moment," he suggested shyly.

The class voted to take turns sitting with the duck, row A first. Ms. Saunders ceremoniously moved Scrawny to the brooder, the big cardboard box where he would grow up. She pretended to play a trumpet fanfare.

Since John sat in row B, he didn't have a turn with Scrawny until spelling. He hunkered down by the box on the floor. A strong bright lamp shone its light into one corner to keep Scrawny warm. John reached in to pat the sleeping yellow duck. He was totally fluffy now. John rubbed the black spot on Scrawny's head. To his surprise, the duck woke up. He stood up and peeped at John.

"Hi!" John whispered back.

The duck walked closer, balancing perfectly on his bright orange webbed feet. He had thin black stripes through each eye and across his cheeks. Scrawny cocked his tiny head from side to side at John, as if he were asking, "Who are *you*?"

John laughed out loud, then remembered he was in class.

Luckily, the recess bell rang. John leapt to his feet. He'd been waiting to play soccer with Andrew again. Yesterday, they had played forwards on the same team. The game had been the first exciting one he'd had all year. He was even hoping that he and Andrew might be friends. He didn't have any good friends here yet. " 'Bye, Scrawny!"

The duck stood up, too. He was chirping loudly. John would bet a fly to a frog that the duck sounded *upset*. John hesitated.

The girls gathered around the brooder. "Isn't he cute?"

For an instant, John thought they meant him. He blushed. Then the girls patted Scrawny and filed out of the room. John sat back down beside the lonesome duck. He guessed that playing soccer with Andrew would just have to wait.

John dangled his hand in the brooder. The duckling pecked at his finger, then got sidetracked and headed for the water trough.

Since John was alone in the classroom, he decided to try an experiment. He sank down on his hands and knees so Scrawny couldn't see him. John crawled silently to the other side of the box. Then he lifted his head. "Duck, duck, duck."

Scrawny peeped and waddled toward him.

John crouched lower and crawled to another edge. He popped his head up again. "Scrawny!"

The duck trotted gleefully over to his face.

John got so involved in his game that he lost track of time. He was down on his hands and knees with his bottom in the air and his head low, just crying, "Peekaboo!" when he heard Andrew's giggle behind him.

John looked at the doorway, embarrassed. He sat up straight, aware that even his neck was turning red.

Scrawny, of course, trotted closer now that he could see John's head.

Emily and Andrew both hurried into the room. "Why, that duck has imprinted on you!" Emily cried.

Ms. Saunders pushed her way through the children. She made John repeat the experiment. All John wanted to do was disappear through the floor or turn invisible, but he followed the teacher's instructions. Scrawny walked toward John wherever his face appeared.

Then Ms. Saunders had Emily try. Scrawny ignored her, collapsing under the lamp and falling asleep.

Ms. Saunders put her hand on John's shoulder. "Looks like you're pretty important to that duckling."

"What does imprinted mean, Ms. Saunders?" Elizabeth asked innocently. John had a suspicion she knew.

John could also tell that the teacher was working hard to keep a straight face. Ms. Saunders explained, "Newborn ducks become attached to the first moving thing they see. Usually the mother. That's why they follow their mother in a line."

"But . . ." Mary said, puzzled. "*John's* not a duck."

Andrew hopped up and down. He pointed at John with both arms. "Scrawny thinks John is his mother!"

3

Class Mascot

For the next few days, every activity in the classroom revolved around Scrawny.

They studied ducks in science and drew pictures of ducks for art.

They wrote stories about ducks for English and acted out *The Ugly Duckling* for a special project.

The walls of room 224 were covered with Scrawny. Pictures and stories overflowed into the hall. The principal, Miss Lacksbury, even stopped by to compliment them. "Wonderful work," she said, not looking at any of their faces. John's mother was an elementary school principal, but John was certain she really smiled at kids once in a while. Miss Lacksbury only looked at

13

children's faces when she was angry. Every kid in Wilson Elementary knew that.

John wrote his duck story during recess on Wednesday. He might not be so good at making friends, but he was great at stories. All the children except Emily kept teasing him on the playground. "Mother, mother, mother," they called. So John had decided to stay inside with the duck. Actually, he was secretly proud to be Scrawny's favorite.

John chewed on the end of his pencil. This was going to be his best story ever. . . .

THE GIANT DUCK by John F.

One morning I saw a giant egg in my closet. The egg cracked, and out jumped a three-foot-high duck! The duck followed me to breakfast. His peep was really loud. The duck must have been very hungry. He ate three boxes of cereal and my big sister's animal crackers.

Then the duck followed me to school. I named him Ducky on the way. When we got to class, Ducky had grown. Ms. Saunders pointed to an empty desk. "Sit down!" she ordered. "And no wiggling."

By recess, my duck was seven feet tall. He could already fly. I let everyone in room 224 have a ride

14

around the playground. Emily examined his wings. Andrew took two rides.

The principal came outside. Miss Lacksbury looked right into my eyes. "Get rid of that duck. And don't come back until you do!"

John stopped writing and nibbled at his eraser. He liked the beginning of his story, but he didn't have time to finish.

That night after dinner John played with his model train set to help himself think. Then he lay down on his bed and continued writing . . . .

I knew I couldn't let Mom find out that the principal had sent me home from school. So Ducky and I headed for the zoo. The zookeeper didn't have a cage big enough for Ducky. I took the duck home and hid him in the garage.

Dad came home. He walked right into the garage to look for a hammer. "AAARRGGGGHHHHH," he yelled. "A monster!"

Our whole family got in a fight about what to do with Ducky. We all went to bed sad. I slept on my windowsill. The duck slept outside in my tent.

The next morning a loud thump woke me up. I ran outside and saw an even bigger GIANT duck

*sitting on my roof next to Ducky. The mother duck
had come back for her baby!*

" 'Bye!" I yelled as the two ducks flew off.

*"Quack! Quack!" Ducky answered, and I knew he
was saying good-bye, too.*

The End!!

John added two extra exclamation points. He raced
downstairs to read the story to his family. They didn't
seem very interested.

"It's too silly," Fran declared.

"The part where the duck sleeps in your tent is
good," Mom called from the kitchen.

His biggest sister, Fay, said, "I still like your magic
train story best." She shrugged, "Hey, Johnny, I haven't
heard you practice your violin yet. Want to play with
me?"

The next day during sharing time, John got up his
courage and handed his story to Ms. Saunders to read
aloud. The class loved the story. For the first time that
year, John got the blue star for the classroom's favorite
story. Ms. Saunders mounted the story on a giant blue
construction paper star and put it out in the hallway
on her Brag Board.

As the week passed, Scrawny's feathers grew

16

stronger. He could flap his way out of children's hands. The children were allowed to hold him if they sat carefully on the floor. Scrawny enjoyed cuddly clothes, like sweatshirts turned inside out. Andrew had brought in the little teddy bear he used to have as a baby. The duckling slept on it.

Each day, the class brought soggy plants for him to eat, and Ms. Saunders gave him chicken mash. Scrawny particularly liked the potato chips that Elizabeth sneaked to him.

Scrawny's chirping and peeping filled the classroom while he was awake. He talked *all* the time, especially when something exciting happened.

Thursday afternoon, Ms. Saunders had them get ready early to go home. Then she made them sit at their desks. "Class," she announced, "how many of you remembered that tomorrow is the day that Scrawny must go back to the 4-H Club?"

Not even Emily raised her hand.

The bell rang, and for the first time in the history of Class 224, everyone left silently. No one said a single word.

That night, John could barely eat his dinner. He remembered Scrawny's birth. He had promised Scrawny that he would make it up to him for naming him that horrible name. This was the time. Scrawny

was happy in their classroom. He couldn't let Scrawny turn into an orphan.

The phone rang. Fran jumped to answer. "It's for *you*, Johnny," she said, amazed.

It was Emily. "What if we convince Ms. Saunders to keep the duck as our pet?" Emily said. "Think of anything you can. I'll write a science report, and I'll call some other kids. Be at school ten minutes early." Then she hung up.

"John's got a girlfriend," Fran crooned.

John ignored her and went to his room to think. It wasn't until the next morning that he got an idea. He brought a giant bowl to school. The kids all gathered on the playground to plan.

As soon as the bell rang, Allie gave Ms. Saunders some flowers, and told her that the WHOLE class wanted her to watch a presentation. She presented Scrawny with a fluffy toy duck and then dramatically clapped her hands.

Andrew danced in, dressed in his duck costume from *The Ugly Duckling*. "Please don't send me away," he quacked. "Please!" He handed Ms. Saunders their *Petition to Keep Scrawny*. The petition had been signed by every child in the room, including Danny. Danny never signed anything, not even his papers.

Scrawny peeped loudly in agreement from his box. He was standing on his new fluffy duck.

Mary suggested that they study the environment that ducks need to survive and build that environment in the classroom.

Next, Elizabeth dropped to her knees and clasped her hands together. "I'll just die without Scrawny!" She stood up, straightening her dress. "My parents said I could take the duck home on weekends, Ms. Saunders."

Now it was John's turn. He set his bowl down on the floor by Scrawny's brooder. "We can give Scrawny everything he needs right here while he grows up . . . even a lake to swim in!" John carefully filled the bowl with the class watering can. Then he arranged a board to slope into the water like a ramp. That way Scrawny could climb out by himself. John lifted Scrawny from his box. Nervously, he set the duckling in the water. What if he sank?

Scrawny waved his tail feathers happily. He peeped and swam. Then he ducked his head underwater. He came up shaking the water and squawking louder than ever. The children laughed with delight. Even Ms. Saunders grinned.

Finally, Emily read her report on how ducks should be with their mothers until they were old enough to

be on their own. "We're all his mother, particularly John."

Scrawny stood on his ramp, preening himself.

"Are you all finished?" Ms. Saunders asked fiercely, but John thought he saw a bit of a smile on her face. The teacher sighed. "All right, I'll go talk to Miss Lacksbury. I don't want a single sound while I'm gone." Then she left the room.

John put his head down on his desk. It seemed like forever before Ms. Saunders returned. She threw open the door. "Children!"

Everyone looked at her, including the little duck. John crossed his fingers and even his big toes.

"We have permission to keep Scrawny until the end of the school year!" Ms. Saunders announced. "He does seem to belong here. Scrawny, the classroom duck, will be room 224's official mascot."

4

The Missing Candy

John set a mound of potato chips on the floor during recess. He never offered Scrawny junk food, but this was a special occasion. Scrawny was three weeks old today. John sang "Happy Birthday" very softly. The duckling folded his wings across his back and peeped along to the song.

"We knew you were up to something," Emily exclaimed from the doorway.

"We sneaked inside," Mary whispered.

"Mothers always give their babies birthday parties, right?" Andrew asked.

John felt his face grow hot as Andrew teased him. Yet he liked being famous as Scrawny's favorite. Groups from all over the school had come to visit

23

Class 224's duck display. The class had drawn posters and written reports on the weeds and bugs that ducks ate. Emily had done a report on the oil in a duck's feathers.

Andrew had brought an extra-wide box from home. It wasn't very tall. They had put John's bowl inside and then filled the space around the bowl with pebbles and a big rock so that Scrawny's environment would be like a stream. The children took turns every day changing the newspapers and his drinking water. At night, Ms. Saunders turned on the light in the corner for warmth.

Scrawny was at his "stream" now, perched on the rim of the bowl. With a loud squawk, he launched himself into the air. The duck flapped his stubby little wings. Then he smacked into the side of the box. All four children groaned.

John figured the duck must have smelled the chips and had been trying to fly out. But he was too little. John scooped Scrawny up and set him on the floor by his potato-chip cake. Scrawny took a nibble, then another. He got so excited that he stepped on the potato chips.

"I brought you something, Scrawny-wawny." Andrew pulled a wiggling thing out of his shirt pocket. He dropped it in front of the duck.

"You carried a worm in your pocket to school?" John exclaimed. But he wished he'd thought of it himself.

The yellow-and-black duckling stared at the grimy worm, his head sideways. Scrawny chirped.

"He's waiting for the worm to talk?" Emily wondered.

Scrawny poked at the worm with his bill. It curled into a little ball.

"Ooohh," Mary said. "He hurt it."

"Worms don't have nerves in their bodies," Emily said. Then she paused. "Or maybe that's lizards."

John reached to save the worm.

"Mother, mother, mother," Andrew crooned at him.

John hesitated. In that instant, Scrawny sucked the worm into his mouth and swallowed. A big lump went down his throat.

"Atta boy!" Andrew hopped up to sit on the teacher's desk.

Scrawny's eyes got round and bulged out in surprise. Then his stomach swelled. John lifted him away from the potato chips. The little duck needed to be sidetracked from any more food.

"Lesson time," John said. Every chance he got, he'd been trying to teach Scrawny a new trick.

John got down on his hands and knees and put Scrawny in front of him. He crawled backward. Scrawny followed his face. As usual, when the duck was too excited he couldn't walk straight. He wobbled along in a curvy line.

Then John stood up. He walked away slowly, letting Scrawny see his tennis shoes. The duck looked around as if he were confused. John crouched down to let Scrawny see his face again. "Scrawny!" The duck started toward him. John stood up and walked.

"You're teaching that duck to follow tennis shoes!" Emily cried.

John nodded shyly.

The little duck scooted under Ms. Saunders's desk. The vent blew hot air in his face. Scrawny hopped back.

"He wants the candy." Andrew draped himself over the teacher's desk on his belly to see better. "Smart duck." Ms. Saunders gave the students treats every time they presented a book report. She kept the candy in her bottom drawer right by the heating vent. Sometimes the candy melted a bit.

"Scrawny, you need to learn how to read, first," Emily said.

John laughed. His sisters would like that joke.

Andrew half opened the little drawer. He was still hanging upside down across the desk. "Shall we each take some?"

John inched closer so that he could see the bowl of candy corn and tiny bags of M&M's. He knew the candy would taste wonderful. But he didn't reach out with his hand.

Emily glared at Andrew. "That would be stealing." Scrawny climbed onto Emily's knee to see better.

Andrew craned his neck. "Aw, it's just four pieces. Ms. Saunders doesn't count every little piece, does she?"

Scrawny leapt onto the side of the drawer. Then he hopped down into the bowl and gobbled up a piece of candy corn. He gulped two more down and speared another before John could even gasp.

The bell rang.

"Ms. Saunders will think we've been stealing!" Mary wailed.

John carried the flapping duck against his belly, back to the brooder. He cleaned the sticky candy off his beak. Andrew slammed the candy drawer. They ran to their desks.

"Spelling!" Emily said. "We have a test this afternoon." By the time John heard the noise of the students in the hallway, the four of them were hard at work at their spelling workbooks. Scrawny was still squawking angrily.

"What are these bits of potato chips doing on the floor?" Ms. Sanders asked as she entered the room. She regarded the four students suspiciously. "And what are you all doing in here studying?" She looked at Scrawny. The duck was hopping up and down. "If only ducks could talk."

John bit down on his lip to keep from turning red like he always did. Mary looked sick to her stomach. Emily scribbled furiously in her workbook. Only Andrew seemed normal. The red-haired boy grinned at the teacher. John wished he could be that brave. Still, if Ms. Saunders found out about the candy, they could really get in trouble.

"The chips must have fallen out of *my* lunch," Elizabeth suddenly howled.

Ms. Saunders wouldn't let her check her lunchbox. With Elizabeth sniffling, the teacher started right in on a science lesson about the anatomy of a duck.

5

Scrawny's Adventure

Late that afternoon, when Ms. Saunders left the room for a minute, Andrew hopped up and sat on her desk again. He held up her favorite pen. "Everybody silent!" he announced, imitating their teacher's voice.

Allie slipped out of her seat to guard the door.

Andrew arranged Ms. Saunders's sweater over his skinny shoulders. He waved a ruler in the air, the way their teacher did sometimes when she was feeling fierce. "Mary, stop wiggling. Now recite your times tables."

John couldn't help laughing. Ms. Saunders never yelled at Mary. Besides, Andrew looked funny wearing the embroidered sweater.

"I'd be a better teacher." Elizabeth marched forward.

Andrew wiggled sideways to get away from her. His leg knocked into Ms. Saunders's pencil holder. Andrew grabbed, but not fast enough. All the pencils and pens clattered to the ground, even the one in his hand.

"Ms. Saunders's favorite pen fell in the vent!" Elizabeth screeched. "I saw it." Then she sat down.

Andrew scrambled to pick everything up.

Allie left her post at the door and crouched beside Nathan in front of the vent. "I can see the pen!" Most of the students in the room, including John, stood up to see better.

Nathan poked in the vent with the ruler. "Oops," he said. "I just knocked it farther in."

"What are you all doing?" Ms. Saunders's icy voice asked from the doorway.

Andrew got sent to sit in the hallway. Ms. Saunders wouldn't even listen to his explanation. She made them all work an *extra* page of math. "My last class gave me that pen as a gift." Ms. Saunders got a screwdriver out of her desk and took the front off the heating vent, muttering.

By the time the final bell rang, John's head hurt from all that multiplying. "Aren't you going to put the vent back on, Ms. Saunders?" Elizabeth asked.

"Later." The teacher didn't look up as she dismissed them. "I have a meeting now."

John hurried to the back of the room to say good-bye to Scrawny. He gave the duck some oatmeal. Then he thought, Don't tell anyone about the candy, okay?

John had a violin lesson, so he had to rush. His biggest sister, Fay, picked him up outside the school.

After dinner, the family put a puzzle together in front of the fire. John's back got warmer and warmer until Fran tapped him on the shoulder. "Hey, sleepy-head, it's time for you to go to bed." John stood up grumpily. It was bad enough having parents tell him what to do, without having his sister order him around.

As John climbed the stairs to his room, he saw Fay sneaking her cat in the front door. Midnight was sup-posed to be an outdoor cat because Mom was allergic to cat fur. His sisters carried Midnight to their bed-room almost every night.

The next morning, John headed for school in the rain. He stood in the middle of his huddled classmates waiting to be let inside the building. April wasn't usu-ally this cold.

Ms. Saunders burst out the front door. She headed right for John. "Yes, Ms. Saunders?" He hurried up the steps.

"I need your help," she said quietly. "Scrawny's . . . "

John felt his heart drop into his stomach, but he didn't say anything.

"Can I come, too?" Emily interrupted, appearing at John's elbow.

Ms. Saunders shivered in her thin red-and-white dress. "I suppose so. Hurry."

John walked inside the building. Instantly, he heard loud, angry squawks. "Scrawny?" He spun around, but the duck wasn't anywhere near. The sound seemed to be coming from beneath John's feet, then over his head. He heard skittering sounds. "Where is he?!" Ms. Saunders grabbed John's arm and hurried him down the hallway.

"Isn't it freezing in here?" Emily asked as they climbed the stairway to their second-floor class-room.

The janitor, Mr. Smitt, stood waiting at their door-way. He had dust all over his arms and in his hair. John thought of him as a friendly old man.

"I came in this morning and heard that duck." Mr. Smitt's eyes narrowed. "I've taken off half the grates in this school looking for that squawker. First I thought it was here, then I heard it down in the kindergarten room."

"Sound echoes," Emily explained cheerfully. "The

vents are round, and the sound—" She fell silent when he glared.

"Naturally, I couldn't turn on the furnace," he said. "Might cook the duck. I even turned off the pilot light. Now we're cold!" He spread his arms wide. He seemed more upset about that than about searching for the duck.

Miss Lacksbury arrived. She looked right into Ms. Saunders's eyes. "How could this have happened? You promised me the duck wouldn't cause any trouble."

John scooted between them into the room. Sure enough, Scrawny wasn't at his stream. "He fluttered out of his box! That's the first time," he said to the principal, hoping it would make her less mad.

John joined Emily at the vent by the teacher's desk. Scrawny must have come over here searching for candy!

"Do ducks have memories?" Emily whispered, looking at the treats drawer.

"One of the children knocked my pen into the vent," Ms. Saunders explained. "I'm afraid I removed the vent cover. I planned to replace it this morning."

Miss Lacksbury folded her arms and shivered. "I refuse to have three hundred and twenty-six children freeze for one little duck. Get him out in fifteen minutes." Then she left. It sounded like a threat.

34

John and Emily crouched down by the vent. "Scrawny," Emily called into the vent. She breathed in and choked badly on the dust.

"You have any potato chips?" John asked Mr. Smitt.

The janitor lifted his hands into the air and left, too.

"We need Elizabeth," Emily wheezed at the teacher. "She always has potato chips."

"You feed that duck potato chips?" Ms. Saunders snapped.

John flushed. He couldn't say he'd only done it once yesterday during the secret birthday party. John put his face up to the vent and called. He hoped his voice didn't echo too much for Scrawny to follow the sound.

Ms. Saunders started tapping a pencil on her desk.

The bell rang. "I have a feeling Scrawny is nearby," John said. "After all. This is his home."

Within minutes, every student in the class was scrunched up around the vent with their lunches . . . everyone except Andrew. He sat in the back with the teacher. "It's not my fault," John heard him cry. Emily wasn't much help either. She had gone for a tissue to wipe the dust out of her eyes.

Nathan offered a cupcake to tempt Scrawny. John leaned forward and squished it under his knee.

"Yuck," Allie said, scraping the chocolate off John's pants. She licked her fingers.

"I'll give you my potato chips for a quarter," Elizabeth offered.

"What?" John felt squashed by all the kids around him. If one more person poked at him, he might scream.

"Oh, Elizabeth," Mary said.

Elizabeth handed the bag over with a loud sigh. John knew ducks could smell, but he wasn't sure how well. He called Scrawny's name and reached down the vent with a handful of potato chips. Nathan jarred him. The chips fell out of John's hand and down the vent.

"It's time to give up," Ms. Saunders announced.

"We can't let the janitor turn on the heat," Emily wailed. John had never heard *her* wail before.

Yet the class obeyed Ms. Saunders and headed back toward their chairs . . . everyone except for John. The sleeve of his green shirt was dark brown with the dust.

"John," Ms. Saunders said.

John still hesitated. He refused to let Scrawny be cooked. Besides, he thought he'd heard something.

When all the other voices were gone, John did hear something. A crunch. A loud crunch. "Scrawny! He's in there, eating the potato chips." John reached in again. "My arm isn't long enough!"

Ms. Saunders was already down on her knees beside

him and reaching in. "Come on, you squirmy little duck." She sneezed. "Ah, I've got you!" Ms. Saunders pulled out a grimy gray ball of fluff.

John hardly heard the joyful noise from the rest of the class. Scrawny wiggled free and headed back toward the vent. John grabbed him, then thought to feed him more potato chips. Quickly, the teacher screwed on the vent cover.

Ms. Saunders had dust in her hair and a streak of dirty brown down her face. Her red-and-white dress was spotted with dark smudges. Ms. Saunders put her arm around John's shoulders. "Well, John Frederick Felix Elijah Forest," she said softly. "We saved our duck." Then she began to giggle a bit wildly. John was afraid she might cry.

At that moment, Miss Lacksbury stepped into the classroom. John and Ms. Saunders stood up. John cradled the filthy duck against his shirt.

Everyone fell silent. Scrawny swallowed his last potato chip and chirped in greeting. To John's relief, Miss Lacksbury wasn't looking at his eyes.

"Humph!" she said. "You two had better clean up." She had an odd expression on her face, as if she were trying to keep from laughing. She pointed. "As for *that* duck . . . "

"Please . . . " Emily whispered from her chair.

All Miss Lacksbury said was, "You'd better clean him up, too!" Then she was gone, closing the door behind her.

John counted to five and then started the cheering.

6

Wilson Elementary's Most Famous Tradition

After Scrawny's adventure into the furnace, Class 224 kept the door to their room closed. Scrawny fluttered out of his stream all the time. He would climb onto the big rock, madly flap his little wings, and hop over the edge of the box. Yet he couldn't fly back in. He would stand outside and quack until someone helped him. The students leaned a ramp against the box so he could waddle back in himself.

Luckily, Mr. Smitt took a liking to the duck. The janitor whistled operas to Scrawny while he cleaned the room.

As Scrawny grew stronger, he learned to clamber onto Ms. Saunders's stool by using his beak. Then he would jump onto the low, wide windowsill. He looked lopsided as his long feathers came in one by one.

On the last day of April, the duck squawked at a crow on the other side of the window in the middle of social studies. Everybody jumped, particularly the teacher. John told the crow story to his family at dinner. Even Dad laughed.

After that, John related a story almost every night. "The Tales of Scrawny," Fran called them. John told how Scrawny slipped out of the room and waddled down the hallway right behind a kindergartner, scaring her. He told about Scrawny racing down the aisle and quacking at Andrew whenever the teacher got mad at him.

The best tale of all was about Scrawny visiting the first grade one day. When the first-graders followed the teacher to art, Scrawny joined them at the end of the line. On the way, he stopped at the pond by the principal's office and ate one of the goldfish.

John couldn't imagine his class without Scrawny now. John still didn't have any good friends, but nobody teased him. Children from all over the school used every excuse to visit. John's tennis-shoe experiment had succeeded beyond his greatest hopes. If a tennis shoe went by, Scrawny would follow, peeping.

Ms. Saunders had started wearing tennis shoes, too, even with her fancy dresses.

On the eve of Wilson Elementary's most famous tradition, Ms. Saunders asked the children to sit back down at the end of the day for a special announcement. "Remind your parents that tomorrow is a half day. Tomorrow is also Dog Day."

John sat on the edge of his chair. Every year, the sixth-graders would read the book *Big Red* and then have a dog show at school. No dogs were allowed inside, but there would be dozens of dogs outside on the playground. John had even heard that the local newspaper took pictures of the event.

"My class always watches the parade from the window," Ms. Saunders said. "I'll have a treat for you."

Scrawny chose that moment to strut up the aisle by John's desk. Scrawny was brown-and-tan-spotted now. His juvenile wing feathers had all grown in evenly. Emily said that shouldn't happen until he was ten weeks old, so he must be precocious. The duck was only six-and-a-half weeks old. Scrawny pecked at John's shoe for attention.

"If you are well behaved," the teacher continued, "you will be allowed to watch the contests. Mr. Ellis, the sixth-grade teacher, has added a new ribbon for the Best-Dressed Dog."

Scrawny waddled on his bright orange feet down the aisle to Ms. Saunders. His tail still looked scraggly. He tilted his head up and squawked at the teacher.

"Yes," Ms. Saunders said. "You may watch, too, Scrawny."

Class 224 spent the next morning talking about different breeds of dogs ... such as sheepdogs, who herd sheep and sometimes ducks ... and Labradors, who are trained to retrieve ducks for hunters. At exactly ten o'clock, John heard barking outside. The dogs had started arriving!

"Let's line up by the window," Ms. Saunders suggested.

John joined the friendly jostling.

"Whooeee!" Andrew cried.

The playground had been transformed into a judging ring. There was also a bake sale, and a table full of ribbons that John knew were for Best Barker, Best Jumper, Best Trick, and the Longest Ears. More dogs arrived.

"My aunt cuts dogs' hair," Elizabeth announced. "Look — there's a Saint Bernard!" To John's surprise, Elizabeth knew more than anybody. She pointed. "That's a Samoyed, the white long-haired, fluffy one. My aunt says they were bred to herd reindeer and little children in Siberia. They make terrible guard

43

dogs because they are so friendly to everybody — even robbers." There were itsy-bitsy dogs, dogs in clothes, and dogs getting tangled up in leashes.

Scrawny stalked along the windowsill.

Elizabeth sniffed. "Most of these dogs are *mutts*."

Scrawny's feathers ruffled. "What's the matter, boy?" Andrew patted him. "You agree with Lizzy?"

Elizabeth gasped. "Ms. Saunders, Andrew called me Lizzy!"

Ms. Saunders was distributing cookies and didn't seem to hear. The parade started. Half the school had gathered outside to watch, but John didn't mind. He could see better than any of them. Scrawny quacked and hopped down off the ledge.

"I'm going to the rest room," Elizabeth declared in a pouting tone of voice.

No one answered. John gobbled his chocolate-chip raisin cookie. The parade circled back. All the dogs and their owners walked in a straight line now. It was a wonderful sight. John wished for the millionth time that he could have a dog, but his mother was allergic to them. He'd never had a pet of his own, not even a gerbil.

"There's an Irish wolfhound." Ms. Saunders pointed to the biggest dog John had ever seen. "They were bred to hunt wolves in Ireland, I think. Elizabeth can tell us when she returns." The music played triumphantly over the loudspeaker as the first of the dogs crossed the finish line.

"There's a Labrador loose in the hall!" Elizabeth yelled.

Everyone instantly rushed toward the hallway. Elizabeth must have left the door open when she went to the bathroom. Luckily, Scrawny was in his stream.

"Spotless, come!" a voice called from downstairs.

John stood up on a desk so he could see over the students by the door. He knew it wasn't allowed. A sixth-grade girl raced down the hallway after her hundred-pound, snuffling black dog. "Don't worry, he always comes," the girl said. "I can't figure out why he's so excited. Spotless, come!!"

"There's a duck in my room, silly," Elizabeth shrieked.

Ms. Saunders stepped out of the classroom. "Young lady, what are you doing inside the school with a dog?"

The girl skidded to a stop. "I . . . I forgot my jacket."

"Smell the duck?" Elizabeth leaned over to ask the dog. John could see her lips still moving. "Duck, duck, duck."

The big dog rushed past Ms. Saunders and a wall of children into the classroom.

Emily yanked John off the desk. "Labradors are a duck's natural enemy!" The two of them raced for Scrawny. The duckling had already leapt into the air, squawking.

The Labrador jumped into the box after Scrawny and flattened it. Scrawny ran across the classroom, his wings flapping furiously. The barking Lab followed. Children screamed and ran to get away. Nathan rolled under his desk.

"Get your dog!" Ms. Saunders demanded.

"I'm trying." The girl moaned. "We're just starting to field-train him. He gets too excited with ducks."

The Labrador craned his neck to watch the duck. Scrawny had scrambled over Ms. Saunders's high-topped tennis shoes, onto her chair, then to her desk-top. He skittered onto the shelf of the adjacent book-case. Scrawny folded his wings and tried to hide behind the dictionary. Spotless raced toward the bookcase with his tongue hanging out. Everyone shrieked, even Ms. Saunders. The Labrador leapt and hit the bookcase with his front paws.

Ms. Saunders yanked Emily away as the bookcase crashed across the doorway. Scrawny landed at John's feet. John grabbed the flapping, terrified bird. Then the dog raced toward them. All of his pointed teeth

showed. John screeched. He threw Scrawny into the air and dived to one side.

The bird disappeared down the hall with the dog behind.

"Is anyone hurt?" Ms. Saunders demanded. "No one move!"

John was already climbing over the bookcase. He heard someone behind him ... the sixth-grade girl. They raced down the hallway side by side.

"Does your dog eat ducks?" he asked.

Scrawny flew down the stairs. At the bottom, he ran, his wings outstretched. The Labrador drew closer inch by inch. He snapped his teeth over and over again. The Lab pulled out one tail feather.

"Oh, Spotless, NO!" the girl shrieked.

Luckily, the main door was open. Scrawny squawked in terror and fluttered out the door. The sixth-grade girl burst outdoors after the animals with John right behind.

Every teacher in the playground seemed frozen. Dogs howled and pulled at their leashes.

Scrawny entered the ring. He fluttered into the air, touched down, then leapt aloft again. John had never seen him fly so well. The dogs in the ring were barking so loudly that John figured they were judging Best Barker. John raced into the ring. A terrier pulled free and ran after the Labrador. A girl tackled her dachshund.

"Spotless!" the sixth-grader screamed again.

John could tell Scrawny was tiring. A row of thick prickly bushes grew along one edge of the school grounds. Scrawny half flew and half scrambled onto the top of the bushes. He turned to face his pursuers. The Labrador instantly launched himself into the air, his mouth open. The little terrier pushed his way into the bottom of the bushes. John felt lightheaded with fear. This was it. Scrawny would be eaten, dog food.

The Lab's teeth snapped shut . . . only inches from Scrawny. Spotless landed in the bushes with a crunch. Then he howled. He couldn't move! His feet didn't even touch the ground. The little terrier yipped and yipped.

Scrawny spread his wings and made horrible sounds, as if he were yelling at the dogs in duck language. John hurried forward despite the pricklers. He reached out for Scrawny. To his surprise, the duck didn't struggle. He cradled the duck against his chest. John wrapped his shirttail around Scrawny to pin his wings. Then he backed out of the bush, scratching his bare stomach.

The sixth-grade girl whispered furiously to her trapped, whining Labrador.

John turned to face a hundred barking dogs. He saw a crowd of parents, all looking at him. John felt his neck and his cheeks and even his ears flush. Worse yet, Miss Lacksbury stood there, staring into his eyes. "It's not my fault," John wailed and burst into tears.

7

One Little Brother
Is Enough

The nurse dabbed Mercurochrome on John's scratches. His belly stung. Then the principal called his mother at her school . . . just because he'd disobeyed Ms. Saunders and raced to save Scrawny. She called the sixth-grade girl's mother, too. Next, Miss Lacksbury marched John to Class 224 and announced that Scrawny had to leave. The class had until next Monday to find him a new home.

Elizabeth moaned the loudest. John couldn't help himself. She had caused this whole thing. Right in front of the principal, he squirted his bottle of glue at Elizabeth's new flamingo sweatshirt.

Miss Lacksbury called his mother all over again.

John went to bed alone that night with his dinner.

That's what happened around his house when he was punished. This was the worst trouble he'd gotten into in his life. John ate his spaghetti on his bed. He had saved Scrawny from being eaten alive by the Labrador. Now the little duck was going to lose his home. It wasn't fair.

By the next morning, John knew that saving Scrawny once wasn't enough. He'd had to move to this town just because Mom had found a good job as principal of a private school. He *understood* what it felt like to leave your home.

John didn't talk at school all day, not even to Emily. He didn't raise his hand once. Ms. Saunders discussed taking Scrawny to the pet shop on Monday if no one found him a home before that. John couldn't think of a single clever plan to save Scrawny. So he went home and called a family meeting.

This was the first time John had ever called a family meeting by himself. Fran and Fay and his parents sat down in the living room. John talked and talked, all the words he'd saved up all day. "When we moved, I still had all of you," he told them. "I'm Scrawny's family. Don't you think Scrawny should still have me?"

"That's a good question," his mother replied.

"But I don't want a duck around here!" Fran cried.

"One little brother is enough," Fay agreed.

John bit his lip and didn't reply. Only his parents counted in big decisions. Mom looked at Dad. Dad sighed. "We'll think about it, son."

John hardly ate any chicken at dinner. He was squishing up his chocolate ice cream when Fay dropped the evening newspaper into his lap. "Your duck is a star."

Right there on the front page was a picture of Scrawny being chased by the Labrador and the terrier. It was a great picture. The dachshund was there, too. In the very bottom corner, John could see the back of his own head. The headline said, "Dog Riot at Wilson."

John took the newspaper to his room. Then he lay in the darkness. He couldn't imagine life without Scrawny. The duck was his friend, his only good friend.

The next two days John hardly talked. He decided that if his parents said he couldn't keep Scrawny, he would sneak over to Elizabeth's house on Saturday. He would take Scrawny and run away. By Friday, John felt so nervous that he'd stopped eating again. Where did people go when they ran away? he wondered.

Late that afternoon, Dad walked into the classroom. He must have left his carpentry job early. "That's my dad!" John yelled, then blushed. Dad had a cage in his arms.

The cage must be for Scrawny! John raced to give his dad a hug and a kiss, right there in front of everyone.

"He's going to be an outside duck," Dad said firmly.

Of course, every kid in Class 224 needed to say good-bye. Emily had the hardest time. She had *tears* on her cheeks as she patted Scrawny. "Can I come visit him?"

John felt too stunned to answer. He had never seen Emily cry. Dad poked him. John felt like patting Emily on the back. Instead, he stuffed his hands in his pockets.

Dad finally answered, "Of course, you may."

"Me, too," Elizabeth cried.

Ms. Saunders handed John the last bag of chicken food. "Take good care of him," she said gruffly.

All the way home, John sat in the backseat with Scrawny. The duck quacked and quacked. Dad drove with one hand on the wheel and the other covering his right ear. "Be quiet!" he finally bellowed.

Scrawny tilted his head and fell silent.

"He's one of the bosses," John whispered to Scrawny.

At home, John helped Dad design Scrawny's outdoor residence. Dad built a little A-frame house for warmth, then enclosed it in one end of a big chicken wire run that gave Scrawny room to walk around. John filled one old bread pan with grain and another with water. Then he pulled Scrawny out of his traveling cage and set him inside the house. "How do you like your new home?"

Fran raced into the backyard. "Hi, famous duck." Scrawny peered out of the A-frame. He tilted his head at Fran and quacked. Fran giggled.

Dad pounded some more wood and chicken wire together. "We'll put a door on for nighttime."

"But Scrawny's never been locked up!" John exclaimed.

"You can let him out every morning," Dad said gently. "It's dangerous for him to be out in the dark, with cats coming around. Not to mention raccoons. Let's put bricks around the edge to discourage the raccoons from digging under the chicken wire."

Fay and Mom came up behind them. "He's a jailbird," Fay said. She bowed. "Glad to meet you, Scrawny."

The duck strutted out of his house. John showed him around the fenced yard until Mom called him in to dinner. Then John watched out the window. Scrawny was still exploring the yard. Suddenly, Scrawny came face-to-face with his sisters' cat, Midnight.

"Oh, no!" John stood up, scraping his chair back.

Scrawny chased the surprised cat. The duck had his wings spread, quacking loudly enough to wake up people for a block in every direction. He tried to nibble Midnight's tail.

"Poor kitty." Fran raced to the door. The cat streaked inside with her tail streaming out behind her. Fay lay down on her belly to coax the cat from under the couch. Midnight's fur stuck out, so that she looked like a black ball.

"That cat belongs outdoors," Mother objected.

"But Mom!" Fay and Fran cried together.

Mom sneezed, but she allowed the girls to carry Midnight to their bedroom.

After dinner, John watched Scrawny gleefully chase a moth across the deck. Then, he hooked Scrawny into his cage.

That first weekend, Emily came to visit the duck three times. She brought duck treats, like carrot peels and even broccoli from dinner. John's mom finally suggested that Emily walk home with him after school every Wednesday. Elizabeth called, but John refused to talk to her. He still thought she'd gotten the Labrador excited on purpose.

His sister Fran started playing rock music to Scrawny to "culture" him. Each spring, the family chore was the garden. Fran spread the manure and fertilizer to the beat of her music.

Dad told John that he was big enough to help this year. He had to turn every bit of the garden over with a spade. Dad expected him to work for an hour after school. John didn't really mind. He would be outside with Scrawny.

Wednesday afternoon, Emily walked home with him from school. They both wore tennis shoes. John noticed because he kept staring at his feet. He'd never really talked to girls other than his sisters. He didn't know what to say. Emily talked about her crystal experiment. "But I'd rather have Scrawny than crystals."

They walked into his backyard. Scrawny came racing to meet them. "Help me dig up the garden?" John asked.

Emily had to jump on her shovel with both feet to make it sink into the earth. Her braid flopped up. John scooped out a spadeful, humming his violin music. Scrawny stood beside him. The duck suddenly leapt into the hole.

"Hey!" John exclaimed.

Scrawny sucked a worm into his mouth and swallowed, just like he had that day of his three-week-old birthday party. After that, Scrawny hopped between

John and Emily, watching every new hole. He ate two more worms and some grubs.

"Scrawny is settling in fine," John said proudly. He didn't say that Midnight stayed out of the backyard now.

"He is?" Emily asked. Something in her tone made John look up. She was looking toward the neighbor's house. John heard a quack. Scrawny was racing along the wire fence that bordered their yard. He had his wings extended. On the other side of the fence raced the neighbor's small dog.

Scrawny came to the end of the fence and stopped. The duck raised up on his toes. He flapped his wings and hissed down at the dog. The dog bared her teeth. Scrawny ran back along the fence, quacking. He looked over his shoulder to make sure the yapping dog was following after him.

John laughed.

"Scrawny must have been psychologically traumatized by the Labrador!" Emily exclaimed.

"He is upsetting Tweetsy on purpose," John agreed. "Scrawny, can't you go easy on that poor, little dog?"

"Tweetsy?" Emily murmured. "Who would name their dog Tweetsy?"

Scrawny stopped to peck the earth. Tweetsy barked frantically and threw herself at the fence over and over, but she couldn't get at the duck.

Emily crouched down in front of Scrawny. "You really hate that dog, don't you? I bet you even have nightmares about dogs."

The little dog was growling, salivating.

"Nightmares?" John joined Emily and Scrawny. Scrawny ruffled his feathers and quacked.

"Better watch him at night," Emily suggested. "Nightmares are terrible."

8

Hide and Seek

John checked Scrawny for nightmares during the next three evenings. The duck didn't make sounds in his sleep. He didn't even move. So John set his alarm on the fourth night and sneaked out his back door at midnight. The silence and shadows made the backyard spooky. John shivered and tiptoed toward Scrawny's house. The duck was sleeping soundly on Andrew's old teddy.

Scrawny might not be having nightmares, but he *hated* the neighbor's dog. He upset Tweetsy almost daily. In fact, Scrawny was turning into a pretty fierce duck. He ruled their backyard. Midnight took to sleeping in the front window box.

Scrawny still wasn't old enough to really fly. Emily

said that would happen at the end of the summer when he got his adult feathers. So Scrawny ran everywhere, his wings outstretched. If he was excited, he fluttered a few feet. He loved to race up on the deck and beg loudly for scraps. "Beck, beck, *beeeck*," John would answer.

Fran accused her brother of talking duck language.

On the last day of school, Ms. Saunders called each student up to her desk alone to hand out report cards and say good-bye. Elizabeth knocked over Nathan's pencils on her way. When John went up, Ms. Saunders gave him his report card. John opened the paper slowly. Two A's and the rest B's. He smiled.

"We made it through the year, John Frederick Felix Elijah Forest," she whispered. "You did well at your studies."

"I just wish I was good at friends," he confided.

Ms. Saunders straightened. She looked hard at him, rather like a hawk. "Maybe you need to wash your eyes out so you can see better." John wasn't certain what she meant, but he went back to his desk happy.

For the first month of summer, John did absolutely nothing . . . except swim and play with Scrawny. He and Emily played hide-and-seek with the duck. They would give Scrawny a treat to distract him and then hide. The duck would search. Emily and John hid behind trash cans and in trees and behind the picnic table. The last person that Scrawny found, won. Soon Emily left to spend the rest of the summer with her grandmother.

So John and Scrawny created a new game, chasing each other through the sprinkler. The duck liked to slurp in the watery grass for bugs. One day, John flung his arms out and put his head back in the "rain." He was wearing his red bathing suit. Mom snapped a picture. Scrawny stood beside him, stretched tall onto his bright orange tiptoes, letting the sprinkler water run over his body. John tacked the picture up on his wall next to the newspaper article.

Besides taking care of his important "jobs," like taunting the dog and begging for scraps, Scrawny spent his spare time out on the deck listening to music from the family room. Then he would stand on one foot and go to sleep, his head turned around and tucked under his wing. As Scrawny grew bigger, he left bigger droppings. John had to hose the deck off every day.

In mid-July, John started soccer camp. The day camp turned out to be "fantabulous," as he told his parents at dinner. He even made a friend named Brian.

Soccer camp was to last two weeks. In the middle of his second week, John came home exhausted. They had played a tournament, and he'd been halfback for six games. "I made a goal, Mom!" he said in the car. "The ball sailed over the goalie's fingers."

His mother was quiet, but that wasn't unusual. When they got home, John opened the door to scoot out. Mom reached over. "Wait a moment, John."

"What?" he said, grinning. "Does Fay have a boy-friend over again and you want me to be nice?"

Mom took a deep breath. "We had an accident today."

John felt his toes grow icy. "Dad?" A carpenter's job could be dangerous.

Mom shook her head. "No — Scrawny. He somehow got over the fence. Tweetsy caught him. He's alive, John, but she bit a chunk out of him."

"Where is he?" John raced out of the car toward the backyard.

"He's in the kitchen," Mom called.

John threw open the door. He wasn't sure his legs would hold him up. Fran was in the kitchen, sitting by a small box. Scrawny lay inside, his eyes closed. He seemed to be having trouble breathing.

"Scrawny?" John asked.

The duck didn't answer. He didn't even open his eyes. John could see the bloody hole on his right side just beneath his wing. "Scrawny?!" he begged.

64

Mom came up behind him. "The vet came. He doesn't think he'll make it, John."

John turned around to face her. "He'll make it." John clenched his hands into fists. "That horrible old dog. She's a murderer!" He felt as if he had a train rushing through his chest. "Scrawny *will* live! You'll see."

John refused to go to bed that night. He spent the whole night by Scrawny's side, humming his violin music to the duck like he did when he worked in the garden.

"He can't hear you," Fran said at breakfast.

John thought he could.

Their friend, Roger, who was a vet, came before the meal was over. "No change," he said.

John refused to go back to soccer camp. By mid-afternoon, he could swear Scrawny was breathing better. Dad came home and carried John to bed like a little child. About eleven at night, John woke up. He found an old medicine dropper in the kitchen drawer and started dripping water into Scrawny's mouth. Then he played his violin for him. John wished he knew some of Mr. Smitt's opera songs. He felt as if Scrawny were hidden, and he was trying to find him with only dreams . . . or maybe with determination. He told stories to Scrawny all night long again.

The vet came the next day. He examined Scrawny.

65

"He's better!" Roger said, amazed. "He might live." He poked John gently. "*You* look dead tired."

For the first time since Scrawny was hurt, John almost cried.

"You should be proud of yourself, John," Mom said. John put his head down and fell asleep right at the kitchen table.

When he awakened, he found himself in bed. "Dinner, sleepyhead!" Fran called as if she were repeating herself. "You've been sleeping for *sixteen* hours."

Sixteen hours?! John rushed downstairs. When he knelt by Scrawny's box, his little friend opened his eyes. He even peeped. "Welcome back!" John exclaimed softly.

John gave Scrawny another dropper of water, then slid into his seat. Dad had prepared his favorite meal — pot roast. John ate heartily, four servings of everything except carrots.

"It's good that Scrawny's going to live," Mom said as she served her chocolate cake with maple icing for dessert.

His favorite again.

John could suddenly tell from his sisters' expressions that the family had been talking while he slept. He put down his fork and held himself so still that he stopped breathing.

"But the neighbors are extremely upset," Mom added. "They're worried Tweetsy might get so excited she'll have a heart attack. We're *all* afraid this might happen. . . ."

John felt that train in his heart again, racing faster and faster. "No," he whispered.

"It's simply too dangerous for Scrawny here," Dad said. John begged his dad with his eyes. Dad swallowed. "I'm afraid Scrawny has to live somewhere else, son."

9

Questions and Answers

The next day, John trudged slowly home after visiting Ms. Saunders. He'd been so furious last night that he'd wondered why he'd worked hard to save Scrawny. John had awakened today knowing that he was glad Scrawny would live. He just wished with all his soul that Scrawny could live with him.

Ms. Saunders had listened to his story. Then she'd said, "Let me do research on how to find a home for grown ducks."

John kicked at a rock on the sidewalk. That's what teachers always said when they didn't have an answer.... "Let me do some research."

He watched the rock bounce into the street. He'd taken responsibility for Scrawny the instant he was born. No one else was responsible. Just him.

Then John thought about the difference between his mom and dad's definition of being smart. He had come up with a great question that had convinced Mom to let him bring Scrawny home from school. Now he had to think like Dad and create an answer that would work for Scrawny forever.

John sighed. He guessed he had an easier time with questions than answers. He wished Emily were here.

When John got home, he carefully carried Scrawny's box outside. They sat together in the sun. Scrawny could hardly lift his head, he was so weak.

The next morning, John awakened to a loud sound. The sky outside his window had that bluish gray color of early dawn. Quacks from the kitchen filled the house.

"Shut up, you brainless duck!" Fran yelled.

John sat up in bed. He figured that if Scrawny wanted to greet the dawn, that must mean he was feeling better. Scrawny kept peeping.

"Be quiet!!" Dad bellowed.

For an instant, the house was silent. Then Scrawny quacked louder, pleased to have someone talking to him.

Good duck! John cheered silently. He heard one of his sisters get out of bed in the next room. Then

Fran shuffled by his open doorway. She never awakened cheerfully. John hurried down the stairs after her, but he didn't let her know he was there.

Fran stumbled into the kitchen in her nightgown. Mom had slipped a top over Scrawny's box. The duck chirped in greeting.

"No, I'm not happy to see you," Fran muttered. "Stop singing, you fool duck." Scrawny gave his loudest peep yet. John peered around the doorway. Fran banged on the side of the box. "How would you like to be dinner? People eat duck, you know."

Scrawny fell silent, probably in shock, John guessed. Fran left the kitchen, sighing. John ducked out of the way. His sister stomped up the stairs. She'd only climbed halfway, when Scrawny started hooting again. John put his hand over his mouth to keep from laughing. The duck did sound like he was singing!

Fran raced back down the stairs and pounded on the box. Scrawny instantly quieted. Yet the moment Fran reached the *top* of the stairs this time, he squawked.

John burst into giggles. Scrawny was *so* smart. He was playing a trick on his sister and winning! The duck quacked louder. John laughed so hard that he fell down on the floor.

"Why you little sneak." Fran ran down and poked

at John with her foot. "It's the middle of the night!" Her voice cracked. "This isn't funny!!"

"He sounds like a rock singer," John cried. "You're the one who taught him to like rock music."

From that day on, Scrawny woke the family up every morning at dawn. Fran started sleeping with pillows over her head. The rest of them ate breakfast early. Their kitchen and family room were really one giant space, connected by a double doorway. John and Fay pushed the family room furniture together each morning as a blockade and let the duck out on the kitchen floor to keep them company. Scrawny enjoyed pecking at their feet until they fed him bits of cereal. His wing dragged on his wounded side.

That week, Scrawny's feathers started dropping out. John worried that Scrawny was sicker, then he remembered that mallards molt in late summer. They lose all their feathers and get new ones. John searched carefully until he saw a new brown-and-tan feather on the duck's wings.

John did think up an answer about finding Scrawny a home. But he didn't admit his idea to anyone.

Two weeks later at breakfast, Scrawny scooted past the blockade of furniture and got loose in the family room. When they tried to catch him, he flapped both his wings and ran, looking back over his shoulder at his pursuers. He fluttered into Dad's reading lamp. The lamp crashed to the floor.

Dad picked up the lamp and stared at John. He didn't say a word. Then he got out the broom to clean up.

John knew the time had come. He took Scrawny outside. Scrawny's wound was obviously healed. John turned on the sprinkler in the backyard on the side away from Tweetsy, and they played.

Ms. Saunders called that very afternoon to see how everything was going. "I need your help," John said. He told her his plan.

"Early morning would be best," she replied.

The teacher showed up the next morning in jeans and a sweatshirt. She looked more like one of his sisters than a teacher. John already had Scrawny in the cage. Even Fran looked sad. The whole family put the cage in the car. John tried not to think as he and Ms. Saunders drove away.

John unhooked the door of the cage when they arrived. Scrawny didn't struggle in his arms. John knew he was the only person in the world who could still carry him.

John got out of the car. If he had to let Scrawny go, Griffin Park was a good place. He stared sadly at the little lake. The lake had a resident flock of wild mallards. John shivered in the early morning chill.

Ms. Saunders put her arm around his shoulders. They walked down to the lake, the only people there. The rest of the ducks were still sleeping on the island. John put Scrawny down in the mud at the edge of the water.

"This is your home now," Ms. Saunders said.

Scrawny pulled up a worm. He plopped gleefully into the water and swam. His bright orange feet paddled behind him under the surface of the water. Then he turned to John with a peep. It was a question.

"That's right, boy," John said. His voice sounded a little rough. "You'll be better off wild. No more neighborhood dogs to bite you. Maybe you'll even find a girlfriend and have a duck family."

Scrawny stuck his head under the water. His tail popped up in the air. He righted himself and ruffled his wings. Then he swam farther away, nibbling on a tasty plant floating on top of the water.

Ms. Saunders tugged on John's arm. "We should go now. While he's busy."

John made himself walk away. He saw Ms. Saunders dab at the corner of her eye the way she'd done that morning so long ago when Scrawny's brother had died. John swallowed again and again.

Neither of them looked back.

John wanted to say something brave like, "Maybe

73

we can come visit him." But his voice wouldn't work. His eyes burned. Just as they reached the car, John heard a muffled sound behind him.

"Scrawny?" he cried.

"Oh no, no!" Ms. Saunders said.

They turned together. The duck stood at their feet. He quacked. John knelt down. "Hurray!" John closed his eyes as Scrawny stretched onto his toes and flapped his wings near his face. "You're a great duck!"

Scrawny sounded furious. John could swear he was yelling, "You forgot me!!" Ms. Saunders sighed.

The duck flipped his wings back and shook his tail. He had a white feather in his tail now and several more new brown feathers. Scrawny sounded proud of himself. "This could have been a terrible mistake," he seemed to be saying.

John agreed, until he saw his mother's face when they drove back into their driveway with the duck. She was pounding apart the old chicken wire run with a hammer.

Ms. Saunders took Scrawny home that night.

The next morning, John and his teacher tried again. They both wore boots instead of tennis shoes. At Griffin Park, John put Scrawny down in the mud by the lake. Scrawny swam out toward the middle. A V-shaped ripple spread out in the water behind him. He

poked his bill in the lake, then lifted his head to let the water run down his throat.

"Let's go!" John whispered.

They only got halfway up the hill before Scrawny waddled up behind them.

"We can't give up," Ms. Saunders insisted. This time they both ran the instant Scrawny ducked his head under the water for a weed. Scrawny followed them, quacking cheerfully at the game.

He quacked so loudly that the other ducks started waking up.

John almost threw Scrawny out into the lake, he felt so desperate. "Hide behind the trees," Ms. Saunders suggested.

She hid behind an oak. John climbed into a pine tree. But Scrawny had played hide-and-seek. He knew the game perfectly. The duck found Ms. Saunders first and squawked at her. "Oh, you crazy duck," she said. "You're too smart."

They gave up for the day. On the way home, Ms. Saunders treated John to breakfast. She parked the car in the shade and left a window partly open so Scrawny would be cool. John ate six pancakes with syrup.

John took Scrawny home this time. He could tell his sisters were delighted. Scrawny was part of the family. The duck quacked in his box through dinner.

Midnight sat on the windowsill and hissed through the window at him.

John got up at dawn to quiet Scrawny. He also had a serious talk with him. "You've got to go," he finally said. "Living in a box isn't any fun."

John and Ms. Saunders went to the park later that morning. They sat on the bank together and watched Scrawny swim. They didn't even try to hide. Soon after they arrived, the other ducks began to awaken. John wondered if Scrawny and the other ducks would get along.

Scrawny ruffled his wings. He swam toward the ducks. Then he paddled away. A couple of the ducks had heads that seemed to be turning bright green with white rings around their necks. Most of the ducks were brown and tan like Scrawny. Several brown ones had grayish wing feathers and blue-black tail feathers coming in. They must be molting, too. Scrawny swam in confused circles. He looked at John and peeped.

"It's all right," John laughed.

Ms. Saunders stood up to see better. "John," she said in an odd tone of voice. "The other young ones already have the beginning of their adult coloring. They're *all* getting their winter feathers."

"So?" John thought that might sound rude, so he

added, "Scrawny is, too." His teacher still seemed upset. "What does that mean that's so important?"

"How could I have missed this?" Ms. Saunders shook her head, then announced firmly, "That means Scrawny is a girl."

10

Scrawny's New Family

Every single morning, John and Ms. Saunders drove Scrawny to the park to swim with the other ducks. Scrawny always followed them back to the car. They took turns taking her home at night. John couldn't get used to the idea that he was a she. Yet there was no doubt. Scrawny's new adult feathers were brown and tan, and fully colored males had gray wing feathers with a glowing blue or purple patch, bright green heads, brown chests, and black curvy tails.

His sisters thought it was hilarious. "I always knew it," Fran said. "Anyone that smart must be female."

John thought about it for hours. How could he care about a girl duck that much? Then as the days went by, John realized that Scrawny was Scrawny. Being female didn't change her personality one bit. She was just as crazy and just as tough and just as much fun.

The tenth day that John and Ms. Saunders took Scrawny to the park was bright and sunny. It was the last Wednesday of summer vacation. John flapped his hat in front of his face to make a breeze.

Scrawny swam around with the other ducks. The last few days, she'd stopped swimming away from the ducks. They'd stopped chasing her, too. Or maybe she'd just learned to stay away from the touchy ones.

A car door slammed. Two young children raced down to the other side of the lake. An older teenage girl followed with a picnic basket.

"Here, ducky, duckies!" the boy cried. Ducks in the middle of the lake stopped swimming and turned to look. Each duck had a circle of ripples around it. The little girl threw a handful of bread in the water, and a few ducks ventured closer. Scrawny paddled behind. The teenage girl set down the picnic basket and sank down beside it on the grass.

A male duck with a bright green head swam closer and snatched a piece of soggy bread. The little girl squealed with such delight that the entire flock zipped away.

"Aw, you ruined it," the boy said, as if he were five

years older instead of only two. "Don't *squeal.*"

The teenager pulled a radio out of her basket and turned it on to a rock station.

"Oh, no," Ms. Saunders groaned. "I hate it when someone disturbs other people's peace and quiet."

Scrawny instantly tilted her head sideways.

The boy threw some more bread. This time Scrawny was the first one there. John wasn't sure whether the bread had attracted her or the rock music. Then John felt his stomach twist strangely. How dare Scrawny like those kids? Scrawny was his duck!

"Let's go," Ms. Saunders whispered.

"Go?" John replied.

"Look at him. I mean her." Ms. Saunders tugged John to his feet. "She's part of that group."

John wanted to race down to the water. He felt an almost irresistible urge to call Scrawny. Yet he could hear Scrawny's quack. She sounded happy. Ms. Saunders dragged at the back of his shirt. "This is our chance."

John walked backward. He could see what Ms. Saunders meant. The little girl threw another handful of bread. The ducks were used to her squeals, now. John sent a silent good-bye to Scrawny.

The duck immediately turned to look at him. John dodged behind a tree. He yanked Ms. Saunders with him. It was as if Scrawny could hear his thoughts. At that moment, another bit of bread splashed in front of Scrawny. The duck gobbled the treat before it sank.

After that, John kept his mind carefully blank. He and Ms. Saunders walked as fast as they could to the car. They jumped in. Ms. Saunders started the car and pulled away. Scrawny was still swimming after chunks of bread. John sank low in his seat so the duck couldn't see him. The car drove through the gates of the park, then down the street.

"Whoooeeee!" Ms. Saunders cried, just like Andrew. "We did it. We finally did it!"

"Yippee!" John yelled, sitting up.

Ms. Saunders thumped on the side of the car.

"Hurray for us!" John said.

"Let's go out for ice cream," Ms. Saunders suggested. "We'll get double chocolate sundaes, even if it is only eleven o'clock in the morning." They hummed one of John's violin pieces all the way to the ice cream shop.

When he arrived home to an empty house, John still felt thrilled. He and Ms. Saunders had achieved the impossible. Scrawny had joined the flock.

John decided to make oatmeal raisin cookies. While they were baking, he searched for the negative of the picture of himself and Scrawny. When the cookies were done, John took his allowance and bicycled to the photo shop. He ordered a giant-size blowup to put on his wall.

The rest of the family arrived home together about five. Fran and Fay had been at the pool. Mom had been at school. They all ate the oatmeal cookies together, then went out to dinner to celebrate.

At the restaurant, Fay held up her glass of water. "To John," she cried. They all drank.

John held up his glass of milk. "To Scrawny. May he forever be happy."

"She," Fran corrected.

A small feeling of sadness grew inside John that night as he slept. He awakened at dawn and dressed. John left a note on the kitchen table, then biked to Griffin Park.

He arrived drenched in sweat. The sun had risen over the hill. John dropped his bike by the empty parking lot. He wanted to be certain Scrawny was happy. On the other hand, he didn't want Scrawny to race over and try to go home with him. John sneaked down closer to the lake, tree by tree. The ducks were just awakening.

John couldn't see Scrawny. What if she was gone? What if something had happened to her? She was always awake by now. John's heart pounded as he hurried closer.

"Hi, John Frederick Felix Elijah Forest," Ms. Saunders whispered.

John jumped. Ms. Saunders stood behind a tree right next to his tree. He grinned at her. He was even beginning to think his name didn't sound so bad.

"I parked outside so Scrawny wouldn't recognize the car." Ms. Saunders looked embarrassed. "I wanted to make sure our classroom duck was all right."

"Me, too," John admitted.

"I guess we're all three a bit crazy," Ms. Saunders said.

John agreed. What other kid would be bicycling to the park at dawn? What teacher would be hiding behind a tree? What other duck liked music?

They watched from behind their trees. Three ducks stretched and plopped into the water, followed by three more. The seventh duck poked up its head. The duck was brown with a white tail feather and a thick black stripe through her eyes and across her cheeks. She stood up and quacked very loudly. John could see that she had bright orange feet. It was Scrawny!

Ms. Saunders danced behind her tree.

Scrawny shook from her wings to the tip of her tail. John wished he could feed Scrawny the potato chips he had stuffed in his pocket. It certainly looked like Scrawny was going to be fine.

John tapped Ms. Saunders's shoulder. "Scrawny isn't our classroom duck anymore. Now she's Scrawny, the *wild* duck."

11

The Tail End

School started four days later. John's new teacher, Mrs. Langley, had the reputation of being the tallest, skinniest, and strictest teacher at Wilson Elementary. Ms. Saunders's class was right down the hall. John stopped in to say hello the first day. The two of them had already agreed to keep visiting Scrawny together every Saturday.

Andrew was in his class again. Emily was, too. John couldn't believe his luck. He told Emily all about Scrawny.

"I guess that's his nature," Emily replied. She had grown over the summer. "To be with other ducks, I mean." She still wore overalls.

"Her nature," John corrected.

Emily gasped. "Scrawny's a girl?!" Her mouth hung open.

John giggled. He'd never seen Emily look so surprised.

Emily snapped her mouth shut. "But that means I didn't study ducks enough."

The second day of school, John picked up a ball at recess. "Hey, Andrew. Want to play soccer one-on-one?"

Andrew looked doubtful. He stopped hopping. "You'll get *slaughtered.*"

"Bet you my dessert for a week that I win," John answered.

Andrew won after all, but John didn't mind. Both of them were sweaty and dirty when they went inside. "You've changed," Andrew said.

John shrugged. "Not me." But he wasn't so certain. He'd had to try hard to make everything work for Scrawny. Perhaps the duck *had* changed him.

One afternoon, Emily joined them. "Can I play?"

Andrew threw the ball on the ground. "No girls!"

"Sure," John said at the same moment. It was two to one, so Emily played. She was almost as good as Andrew and definitely a better sport. John had a suspicious feeling that she'd go home and study the game from a book and beat them both on strategy.

The first month of school passed.

Emily did study soccer, but she didn't beat them. She wouldn't play every day. She liked tetherball at recess more.

One day in early November, John stopped at Emily's desk on his way back from the pencil sharpener. "Want to go with Ms. Saunders and me to see Scrawny this Saturday?" he whispered. "Wear a heavy coat. It will be cold."

Emily got over to his house at six-thirty on Saturday morning. John showed her the giant picture of Scrawny and him playing in the sprinkler. Mom had framed the picture and hung it over his desk.

John and Emily played his new computer game until Ms. Saunders arrived fifteen minutes later. "Emily!" she exclaimed. "What a surprise! How good to see you."

John hopped in the car. It *was* good to have Emily along. Then John remembered how nervous he had felt with her last year, just because she was a girl. He'd had a friend all along, and he hadn't even noticed. It had taken him a long time to realize that it was her personality that mattered. Just like Scrawny's.

John hoped he'd never forget.

He had two friends this year, Emily and Andrew. Ms. Saunders was his friend, too. John grinned. Actually, he had four great friends, Andrew, Emily, Ms. Saunders, and Scrawny. Four friends was enough for anybody.

They drove through the gates into Griffin Park. Emily had brought apple peels, and John had brought Scrawny's new favorite treats, cheese crackers.

Scrawny came over to see them the moment she woke up. She gobbled the treats. Then she sat and preened while John and Ms. Saunders hummed the *William Tell* overture. Scrawny couldn't sit still for long. She waddled back to the water.

John noticed that all the ducks seemed restless. In fact, there weren't as many ducks as usual. The back of John's neck prickled. Suddenly, three ducks jumped almost straight up into the air and flew around in a circle. They landed in the lake again with a big splash.

The ducks squawked louder than John had ever heard. Nearly half the ducks were brightly colored drakes. The flock took to the air again and flew right over them . . . all the ducks except Scrawny.

Ms. Saunders gasped. John knew she'd understood.

"They're getting ready to migrate!" Emily exclaimed.

John leapt to his feet and raced down to the water. "Go with them, Scrawny," he yelled, making shooing

motions with his arms. "They're going south where it's warm."

The flock of ducks circled over the lake.

John felt Emily and Ms. Saunders standing beside him. "Go on!" Ms. Saunders encouraged.

Scrawny leaned back on her tail in the water and flapped her wings at them. She was waving good-bye. John was sure of it. With three awkward slaps of her wings against the water, Scrawny took off. She joined the other ducks in the air. The ducks circled over their heads one more time. The flapping of the wings sounded like a rush of wind before a thunderstorm hit. After a moment, John couldn't tell which duck was Scrawny anymore. He felt strangely proud of himself, more satisfied than he'd ever felt in his whole life.

John sighed. He had a great story to tell at dinner that night . . . his last tale of Scrawny.

Then again, maybe he'd see Scrawny next year.

"Ducks usually come back to the same place year after year," Emily said as if she were reading his mind.

The ducks' bodies looked thick against the fall sky. Their wings looked strong, too. John took off his wool cap and tossed it into the air. "Good-bye, Scrawny!!!" he yelled. The ducks spread into a shape like the tip of an arrow. Then they disappeared into the gray, distant sky.